A DIFFERENT VIEW

To Pat, my longest Best Friend, thanks for putting up with me all those years. This is for Us, cheers!

Also, don't I write like a serval killer? lol

Desmond

A DIFFERENT VIEW

Desmond Sallah

Copyright © 2020 by Desmond Sallah.

ISBN: Softcover   978-1-6641-2910-8
            eBook   978-1-6641-2909-2

All rights reserved. No part of this book may be reproduced or transmitted in any form or by any means, electronic or mechanical, including photocopying, recording, or by any information storage and retrieval system, without permission in writing from the copyright owner.

This is a work of fiction. Names, characters, places and incidents either are the product of the author's imagination or are used fictitiously, and any resemblance to any actual persons, living or dead, events, or locales is entirely coincidental.

Any people depicted in stock imagery provided by Getty Images are models, and such images are being used for illustrative purposes only. Certain stock imagery © Getty Images.

Print information available on the last page.

Rev. date: 09/03/2020

To order additional copies of this book, contact:
Xlibris
844-714-8691
www.Xlibris.com
Orders@Xlibris.com
819204

CONTENTS

Forethought vii

Ohio 1
Smithsville 9
Township of King... 15
The Neutral Zone 19
The Savage Lands 24
The White Zone 28
Our Hero... 42
Ohio Again... 45

FORETHOUGHT

Don't let all   the racism and
Murder porn we see everyday make you forget that
There are some amazing white people out there. Though they will
never experience what we go through daily, some at least try to
relate. There are bad apples in every race; they shouldn't
have to kiss our feet or us protest and riot.
Just change the system, it's the
Only thing we've ever
Really ask
For.

P.S. I'm not a professional writer, don't be too judgmental of this. Enjoy.

OHIO

This story is about a middle-aged man named Robert (imagine Bruce Willis). He is a loan officer in a predominant African American neighborhood. For work, he puts on a good appearance, smiles, and does his job, but Rob is really a racist judgmental asshole. Rob and his coworker Hank spend the workday sending messages to each other, usually making ignorant comments about costumers of obvious ethnicities, denying costumers for loans even though they are fully eligible, then making jokes about their misfortunes. At lunchtime is when they engage in racial offense and talk about costumers who tried getting more loans, and today is no different from any others.

"Hey, Rob, you hear about that rapper who got shot? Man, when will these niggers learn?" says Hank.

"They say they want to get better, but all these gangbangers and drug dealers do is kill themselves, their fucking animals," says Rob.

"Yeah, and another one got shot up in an upscale neighborhood. He was trying to rob a house," says Hank.

"Exactly! Only reason he was in that neighborhood was to steal something. Fucking niggers," says Rob.

As Rob makes that comment, an African American worker named Jasmine walks into the lunchroom. She hears the comment and chooses to ignore it as she walks past the two to go to the fridge where her lunch is. After grabbing her lunch, she heads to the coffee machine and pours herself a cup. As she is pouring a cup, Hank says under his breath but just loud enough for everyone to hear, "Jeez, take in the smell on this monkey."

Rob laughs, and Jasmine storms out of the room. Rob and Hank then continue to laugh together.

After work, Rob takes the bus home. Along the way, the bus stops and picks up a gypsy woman and her daughter who appears to be sick. As the bus drives along, the little girl starts coughing. This irritates Rob, so he tries holding his breath and releasing small bursts to breathe. Suddenly, the gypsy woman starts praying for her daughter in her language, which really irritates Rob and sets him off.

"Hey, keep your voodoo chants to yourself. I just had a long day and would like some peace and quiet!" Rob screams at the woman.

"Sorry, I was just praying for my daughter. Relax yourself," the woman responds.

"You don't tell me to relax myself. Maybe if you knew what a hard day's work was, you would have more appreciation for others," Rob ignorantly states.

"You, excuse me! I'm a nurse, asshole!" the woman responds.

A Jamaican woman turns around and interjects, "Everyone calm down! The bus is for everyone. If you don't like it, don't ride it!"

"Shut the fuck up, you jungle bunny. No one asked you for your opinion. I was just trying to enjoy my time after work. Now I got to deal with demon god chants and monkeys, Jesus Christ!" Rob responds.

At this point, the bus driver, who is African American, has had enough of what he is hearing and decides to kick Rob off the bus. Everyone claps, and he gives them the finger as they drive along and leave him behind. At this time, he is only a few blocks away from his stop anyway, so he walks the rest of the way home.

Rob gets home, enters, and closes the apartment door. He throws his jacket on his sofa and goes to the kitchen to grab a beer and make dinner. In his apartment is a big red rug with a swastika in the center. On top of his rug is a coffee table with a demonic statue, gun magazines, a full ashtray, and empty beer bottles. He has a noose hanging on the center of the wall as if it were art. He has a poster of Donald Trump and a picture of him and his family. He also has needle-worked sewed art that says, "Kill the Niggers," looking so elegant but really racist. Rob grabs a beer and takes a swig after he puts his microwavable dinner in the microwave and turns it on. While waiting for his food to warm, he returns to the living room and turns on the television, then sits on the sofa. He starts flipping through the channels and stops on the news, where an African woman is ranting about something.

"I'm sick of all the abuse and murders. Why did my son have to die? And that cop gets to go home comfortably to his family? Without any care or concern? Quinton was a good boy with a good job and a family with kids. How they say wrong place, wrong time? A black man jogging in a white neighborhood shouldn't be a crime!" the woman on the TV says.

Rob, irritated by this and changes the channel to sports, gets his dinner and starts eating. He soon falls asleep on the couch and falls in a deep sleep.

Rob, in dirty raggedy clothes, wakes up in the later hours of the night on a dirty couch in a dirty apartment. In total confusion, he gazes around the apartment and quickly realizes he isn't in the same place he fell asleep. He smacks his face. "No, this can't be real, wake the fuck—"But no change. He gets up and looks out the window, and he sees he is in a broken-down town, not where he lives, and barely anyone in sight. In the distance, he sees someone warming themselves up over a canister fire and decides to go to him to see if he can answer some of his questions. Rob makes his way out of the apartment and heads down the stairs and onto the street. He makes his way over to the stranger and asks the homeless African American man his questions.

"Excuse me, bro, do you know where we are?"

"What's wrong with you? You drunk or something?" The homeless stranger turns around and notices Rob. "Oh god, stay away from me. HELP! HELP!" the man screams.

Rob throws his hands up, palms up, and says, "YO, RELAX! I'm not going to hurt you. I just need to know—"

The stranger wills out a pipe and swings at Rob but misses Rob. Rob decides to get away from this maniac and takes off running. People are starting to come out of their hiding places and see what the commotion is.

"HE'S WHITE! I SEEN HIM!" the homeless man yells.

More people start coming out and looking around. By this point, Rob has taken off. A few blocks away, Rob cuts into an alley and catches his breath. In the distance, you can hear people talking.

"What the hell is going on? Man, you're seeing things. Ain't no one here," says a civilian of the neighborhood.

"I saw him. He spoke to me up close to my face, and he was white as a snowflake!"

Rob takes off running again.

"It was probably a light skin, Frank. Stop smoking," says the civilian.

Eventually, Rob makes his way into the suburbs of a town called Smithville and continues walking down the street. Everything looks so futuristic, and he is in total awe until engaged again by a group of seven African American teens.

"Sweet Christmas! Are you guys seeing what I'm seeing?" says one of the teens.

"Oh my gosh, is that a white man, in our hood?" another one says, and the teens head down the driveway to confront Rob.

"Eh, man, you lost or something? Where's your collar?" ask one of the black teens.

"Actually, I am. I woke up in this shithole apartment, and I don't really know where I am," replies Rob.

"You need to leave them drugs alone, you crackhead," says a teen.

"I don't do drugs," Rob replies.

"Well, you gotta be crazy to be here, late, and without a collar," says one teen.

"Collar? Look, I'm just trying to find a phone, bro. If you could help id—"

A teen cuts off Rob. "I ain't your *bro*!" says the teen loudly.

"Look, I don't want any trouble. I just need a phone," explains Rob.

"Why? So you can call your boys," a teen says.

"Na, it's not even like that, bro."

"I said I'm not your bro!" a teen replies.

"Okay, look, I'll just be on my way. There's no need for problems," Rob says nervously.

"Na, you ain't going nowhere. What's in your pockets though?" a teen asks as they all move in closer.

One of the teens starts patting Rob down, feeling if anything is in his pockets. Rob pushes him and says, "BACK OFF!"

A teen on the side of Rob sucker-punches him, and the teens begin kicking and hitting Rob. An older lady sitting at a window hears the commotion happening outside her window and decides to call the police.

While Rob lays beaten on the floor, the teens start checking his pockets. One of the teens then says, "Yo, drag him to the woods. Someone go get the rope out of my dad's shed," and one of the teens heads back to the house while the rest drag Rob into a forest area.

The teen who went back has run back and meet up with the group. "Let's hang him from this tree," one teen requests, and they prompt Rob up and put the rope around his neck, not a noose, but it will do.

While # teens hold Rob, four pull the rope and yank Rob up in the air. He dangles there for a few seconds, but then the rope breaks. Rob lands weakly half standing and takes off in an explosion of adrenaline. The teens chase after him; they go up the path and back onto the street. At that moment, the cops show up, and the teens scatter. Rob drops to his knees and catches breath.

"Oh—oh god—thank God you guys are here," says Rob as two officers exit their vehicle, one Spanish and the other African American.

"What seems to be the problem here?" asks the Spanish officer.

"Oh god—I thought they were going to kill me," says Rob.

"Why, what did you do?" asks the Spanish cop.

"Nothing, I was just minding my own business."

"Oh, it's because their black then, eh?" asks the African cop.

"No, no, they attacked me!" says Rob.

"Oh, playing the victim, eh?" says the Spanish cop.

"No, I'm not, I'm just lost," says Rob.

"You do any drugs tonight?" asks the African officer.

"No, I don't do drugs. Jeez, what's wrong with everyone?" Rob responds in an irritated voice tone.

"CALM DOWN, OR I WILL PEPPER-SPRAY YOU. DO NOT THREATEN ME!" says the African cop.

"We're just doing our jobs. We have family to go home to too, buddy," says the Spanish cop.

"I'M NOT THREATENING YOU!" Rob yells back.

The African cop then gets on his radio and says, "Ten-four, we have suspect in custody."

"CUSTODY? WHAT AM I BEING ARRESTED FOR? I haven't done anything wrong!" states Rob.

"Sir, please put your hands on the car," says the Spanish cop.

"I DIDN'T DO ANYTHI—"" screams Rob as the two officers grapple with him to put on the handcuffs.

"SIR, STOP RESISTING!" says the African cop.

The cops then throw Rob against their squad car, and Rob, with full privilege, decides to still yell at them. As he turns around to further engage with the officers, the Spanish cop pulls out a baton and hits Rob in the shoulder and in the ribs. Rob goes down for a second then pushes him down and takes off for his life. The African cop checks on his partner then takes off after Rob, who has made a good distance in a short time. The cop shoots at Rob but misses. Rob then makes a sharp turn and starts hopping fences. He hides in a big-sized doghouse and tries to catch his breath, but because of all the noise, the dog comes outside from a doggy door and chases him out of the backyard. The cop a couple backyards back and in the wrong direction hears the dog and heads that way. Rob takes off, barely escaping the dog, and ends up in a backyard with a shed after jumping a few more fences and decides to hide in the shed. A motion-detector light turns on, and inside the house, a small dog is woken up from the shed door closing. The little Pomeranian exits through his doggy door and investigates after noticing the light on. The dog walks to the shed door and sniffs around, then starts barking. Inside the house, an African American couple is woken up by the dog's barking.

"Ugh, why is Marley barking? Go see what's wrong with him, honey," says the wife.

The husband (imagine Samuel L. Jackson) jokingly says, "Dammit, you know I only got that dog to impress you. We really don't need him anymore."

"Just go see what's wrong," says the wife.

The husband gets up, puts his robe and slippers on, and heads down the stairs and outside to check the commotion. As he gets to the back door, he sees the dog barking at the shed, so he grabs his bat that he keeps by the door. He cautiously heads out and approaches the shed.

"WHO'S IN THERE? COME OUT NOW!" says the man.

"I'm sorry, I'm not trying to cause problems, I just need help, I'm lost," say Rob.

"Well, damn, you're in my shed. There's more light out here, asshole," says the man.

"No, I mean I'm not from around here, I don't know where I am," says Rob.

"Well, come on out, and we can talk more," says the man.

Rob opens the door and shows his face.

"SHIT! Stay right where you are, don't come any closer," the man says petrified.

"Please, I'm not going to hurt you, I just want to go home," pleads Rob.

"What are you doing here?" asks the man.

"I don't know where I am. I woke up in this strange place and dirty clothes. I live on Lakeview Street in Ohio. This clearly isn't Ohio," says Rob.

"OHIO? Are you crazy? Ohio hasn't been around for decades."

"What?" Rob says in disbelief.

Just then, police sirens pull up to the house. It's the two who are chasing Rob.

"Please, help!" Rob pleads.

Confused, the man looks back and then tells Rob to go back into the shed, which he does, and soon after, the two cops enter the backyard.

"Good evening, sir, sorry for bothering you, but we're looking for a dangerous savage that was spotted in the area, followed him into the backyards and tracked him in this direction. See, saw your backlight on, so we're just here to make sure everything is in order," says the African cop.

"Really? That strange, this is such a good neighborhood. I haven't seen anything, just taking the dog out," replies the man.

"Kind of late, no?" asks the Spanish cop.

"Weak bladder, trust me when I say they're both bitches. Plus, it's better out here than on the first steps on my carpet," responds the man.

"Okay, sorry to bother you, sir. Have a good night," says the African cop.

"You too, hope you find him," says the man, and the cops leave. The man waits for the cops to get in their car and takeoff before telling Rob the coast is clear and to come out.

SMITHSVILLE

"Thank you. You honestly don't know the night vie been having," says Rob.

"Well, it's not over yet. You're lucky I believe in equal rights. Let's go inside and figure this out. You're not crazy, are you?" the man responds.

"NO, not crazy, just a crazy night," Rob responds, and the two and the dog head inside the house. "Please, do you have water?" asks Rob.

"Sure, sure," says the man as he gets Rob a bottle of water from the fridge.

Rob chugs the bottle to halfway, then asks, "What do you mean Ohio hasn't been around for decades?"

"Ohio is the old state name for New Ghana. It changed after the race war of 2025. Jeez... you don't look like you're on drugs, but it's crazy you wouldn't know that," says the man.

"2025? What year is it?" asks Rob.

"The year is 2068," says the man.

Rob is shocked, but it all makes sense now, the futuristic houses, the advance technology for streetlights, and what not.

"Like I said, I'm not from here. I'm forty-eight years in the future," says Rob.

"Bullshit! You're a time traveler? You expect me to believe you're from the past? Who are you, Sam Jones from ***Quantum Leap***?" asks the man.

"No, I'm a loan advisor," says Rob.

"Come again?" asks the confused man.

"No, I mean, my name is Rob. I don't know what quantum leaper is," replies Rob.

"Rob, eh? Well, you don't seem like you're on drugs, so my name is Cameron, but people call me Cam," he says.

"What is it with everyone asking me if I do drugs?" asks Rob.

"Don't be mad at me. History speaks for itself. Shit, if that bothers you, then knowing white people are the minority now will piss you off, huh?" says Cam.

"What do you mean the minority? Shit, it finally happened, huh? You mo—I mean, people—have finally taken over the planet?" says Rob.

"Uh yeah...yeah, ethnics are the majority now. Shit, you're serious eh?" asks Cam.

"I'm from 2020.Shit was bad, but it wasn't this bad," says Rob.

"Actually, things are better! Besides a few bad apples, we've pretty much achieved world peace... There's no more wars, cannibals and molesters aren't in power, and animal life is thriving. I read about 2020 in the history books. I don't know how you all survived," says Cam.

"World peace, my ass, I almost got killed tonight just for being white," replies Rob.

"Yeah, racism is still around, but it's directed more toward whites more than other races. History has shown the white people in power isn't the safest direction for the planet. Most people nowadays discriminate against whites. People call them savages now because Caucasian just wasn't doing it. To live among the ethnics, you have to wear a judgment collar for five years as a trail-run test. If you prove you're peaceful, you won't need a collar, and you will get a tattoo badge on your neck," explains Cam.

"That's a bit harsh, don't you think?" asks Rob.

"Hey, I don't make the rules. I just support safety for all," says Cam.

"That's some racist bullshit!" says Rob.

"Well, if you don't like it, you can always go to the White Zone. It's just past the Savage Lands. Pretty self-explanatory, really, if you ask me," says Cam.

"Really, eh, so why did you help me then if I'm just a 'savage'?" asks Rob.

"Because unlike some others, I believe in equal rights and equal opportunity. I saw fear in your eyes and not a buzz. Despite what you might think, some people actually want to help others," says Cam.

"Well, it seems I'm not wanted around here, so how do I get to the White Zone?" asks Rob.

"Well, it's about three cities over to the south. Every state has one. That's where most white folk were forced or chose to live. We gotta get past the Township of King, the Neutral Zone, and the Savage Lands."

"We?" asks Rob.

"Well, hell, it wouldn't be right sending you off on your own with no sense of security. I wouldn't be able to sleep," says Cam.

"I appreciate that," replies Rob.

"Now I can get you through King and TNZ, but you're on your own through the Savage Lands. Ethnics aren't really liked there. You wouldn't be safe either. It's everyone for themselves basically, true savages, mainly cannibals, criminals, and rapists," explains Cam.

"And here I thought world peace would make us one big happy family. Well, at least you're here for me, brother," says Rob.

"Um, you might want to cool it with that 'brother talk.' We aren't brothers, we are strangers, and calling me brother doesn't make you relate to me in any way," says Cam.

"Noted, can we make our way now?" asks Rob.

"No, it's pretty late, best for us to get some rest and leave early in the morning. I'll leave a note for my wife, and this shouldn't take all day. Still, I don't know you, so please excuse me for being cautious, but you have to sleep in the garage. It's not a castle, but it's better than a shed," responds Cam.

"Sure, whatever," says Rob, and the two head to the garage, and Cam leaves Rob there, and he soon comes back with a pillow and a couple of blankets for him to sleep on. Rob makes his bed on the floor next to a futuristic-looking car; his mind is filled with thoughts but, eventually, manages to fall asleep.

As the sun rises, Rob is woken up by Cam who has an egg sandwich and a juice box for him. He explains that Rob will have to sit in the back and cover his neck to hide he doesn't have a tattoo. He will look like a slave and have to pretend to be Cam's slave, an occupation white people can attain voluntarily. White people have done some of the worst atrocities in history, so judgment collars are a way of protecting a mass shooting or worse. Since he doesn't have one, he will need to cover up. The two get in the car and head out on their way. While on the drive, Rob asks why whites were pushed down south.

"Most whites were forced south in retaliation of a little girl dying in a house set on fire in 2030 for no reason except racism. They gave them chances after the race war, but the more we forgave, the more they did. They raped, murdered, looted, had racist rallies, etc. We couldn't move forward like this. We all realized we wouldn't come to a peaceful agreement, so they got pushed south, and southerners came up to the better climate," Cam explains.

Rob is silent.

"Oh, nothing to say?" asks Cam.

"We aren't that bad," replies Rob.

"Not all of you. Realistically, every race has its bad apples, but it is what it is. Your art is satanic, so is most of your suicidal rock-and-roll. Y'all are excited by violence and blood. You deny your homosexual tendencies, and the funny part is y'all lived great lives. It's quite ironic. And for those reasons, we, the people of color, need to know who's crazy or not," explains Cam.

"We were expressing ourselves."

"Well, so was NWA, Public Enemy, Wu Tang Clan, all the musical artists from the past, but the more they said, the more they used it against them," says Cam.

"Well, in my time, you're all drug dealers and gangbangers. No one's perfect. You make your own reality," replies Rob.

"Um no...The system of the past made our reality. It worked against people of color. We never stood a chance. We had to work harder, pay more, barely get work, and still have to pay ridiculous bills. And no matter how hard we tried, we would be called lazy and untrustworthy. Only other option to survive was illegally," explains Cam.

The two pass a sign that says Township of King on it.

"Okay, we are approaching King. Are you ready for this?" asks Cam.

"Yeah, I can't believe I'm a slave," says Rob.

"Relax, slaves are common these days, difference is we don't whip them. We just take points away. With enough points gone, you get fired. It's a way to pay us back for the sins of your ancestors," explains Cam.

"Anything else I should know about?" asks Rob.

"Well, history has proven white people like to play organic wolf."

"Wait, organic wolf?" asks Rob.

"One thing at a time. Anyways, due to the people referred to as 'Karens,' the new government has passed the Emit Till Law—anyone who lies about a crime involving race gets an automatic ten years in prison. Also, rapists get public hangings, molesters are castrated, and poachers die from a firing squad funded by PETA. That's more for trophy hunters and unnecessary death, so don't do any of that shit," explains Cam.

"No problem, to be honest, that doesn't sound too bad. I actually agree," replies Rob.

"You'd think so, huh? It took seven years for the laws to actually work, and you know how hard it is charging a person in power with money? They paid high prices to try and hunt secretly out of spite or to rebel—another reason whites are called savages. So everyone has gets accordingly—the richer, the more taxed. But nothing too crazy, our system works," states Cam.

"Yeah, for everyone, except whites. It's like you think whites are the only ones who do crime," Rob says.

"No, no, there's bad in all races, but not all races do the same crime. Robbing is one thing, murder is another. Worst thing that could happen is being charged as a savage. That's banishment," Cam responds.

"Still, crime has no color," says Rob.

"Yes, it does, it's white! After laws got passed and events took place, most of the planet followed the peaceful way. Living became more peaceful and stress less. We banned nuclear weapons, cleaned the oceans, restored nature... We fixed the planet," Cam says.

"Well, it seems it only got worse for white people," Rob states.

"Well, hell, the patterns of history has proven itself, and if there's a pattern, there's a problem. It took years to piece together real history. In 2027, the Vatican was raided, and hidden documents were finally released. Turns out, most of history was a lie. Black history didn't start with slavery, we were a happy people before that, and we are a happy people now. It's not like there isn't white people around. There's plenty, they just needed to do a mental stability test to prove they aren't a danger to society. No mass shooters, no terrorists, no potential psychos, no extra privileges. Just good behavior," Cam responds.

TOWNSHIP OF KING

The two enter the Township of King, and Rob is in awe of how beautiful it is; children playing in parks, people walking their dogs and greeting one another, beautiful buildings, walkways, and statues. People of all races are here, including whites, some without collars and some with. Rob notices the huge blinking collars and is intrigued.

"Hey, I thought you said white had to wear a collar. I was thinking like a dog's, but what are those?" asks Rob.

"Oh, those are the judgment collars white have to wear for five years. It's to let people know you're not a danger. If you are, the green light rapidly blinks red for a short time before shocking you unconscious. It measures adrenaline and chemical imbalances for a good while. If it decides you might be a danger, it activates, and you are on a probation period. If you do prove to be a danger to yourself or society, it sends a controlled shock to your system to knock you out until the police come and take you for reevaluation," Cam says.

In shock, Rob stares at Cam and says, "Shit, isn't that a bit much?"

"Not if you're level-headed. Everything can be talked out until it can't, right? At worse, you can always walk away too, right? Besides, there was a time when people enjoyed human zoos of black adults and children. They played 'hit the nigger, baby,' and whatnot. Putting yourself in the shoes of your enemies will humble you real quick, as they say," replies Cam. "Also, those places you called zoos don't exist anymore. We have sculptures and videos in museums. It's equal rights for all, including animals and whites, if they prove they aren't dangerous. Even when you go to the White Zone, you can always come back and give peace a chance, if it's not to your liking. We try to be fair," adds Cam.

"What about that place I woke up in, that place didn't seem so lovey-dovey?" states Rob.

"Yeah, every good place has its bad places. That part of town is full of junkies, alcoholics, and basically people who gave upon life. They are looked down upon in society, so they go where they can be among themselves. It's better that way. We wouldn't want them under the eyes of Jackson," says Cam.

"Statue of Jackson?" asks Rob.

"Yeah, Michael Jackson, it replaced the falsified Statue of Liberty. There was no liberty back then, and MJ is an angel, voice of an angel too!" explains Cam.

"Wasn't he a child molester?" asks Rob.

"That was never proven. What was proven was the existence of the Illuminati, propaganda through news outlets, and mass manipulation through Hollywood. Signing a contract was selling your soul to the devil… Molestation, drugs and alcohol, sleepless nights, they drained them dry 'til they died, then you would label them a legend when really they did nothing to benefit society. Some might have been legends, but most weren't, in my opinion," says Cam. "Ah, here's the statue now," says Cam as they cross the bridge over water that exposes the Michael Jackson Statue. It's the same one from the *HIStory* album, standing where the Statue of Liberty used to be. From the looks of it, King is a rich town with happy citizens, performers, buskers, food vendors of all sorts.

"Wow, this really is a beautiful place, Jesus Christ, this is paradise," Rob states.

"Um, that's another thing—a lot of that Jesus story was just manipulation and twisted words. We don't praise him anymore. Black people have woken up. The man you all praised was Cesar Borgia, the song of a pope and closet gay. We ended all things supporting the gay agenda. Gays exist and are accepted, but it's more of a personal choice than mass manipulation. Before slavery, we had many gods—gods of the sun, moon, corn, misfortune, etc. We've gone back to those ways. Anyways, now we praise Saint Badu...just feels good saying her name. She's the saint of good fortune," says Cam.

"Yeah, well, I ain't one for religion anyways, I'm glad it's gone," replies Rob.

"Oh, religion exists ... If you want to talk universe, we are talking about one God and ONE GOD ONLY...Creator of all, good and bad, left and right, night and day, Alpha and Omega...That's the big boss," Cam replies.

"Let me guess, Tyler Perry?" says Rob.

"God doesn't have an image. He is everyone and everything. If the soul is good, it represents the power of the creator," says Cam.

"Can't argue with that. Yaay for Saint Badu," replies Rob.

"Close enough," says Cam jokingly.

"Hey, what's that?" asks Rob as he sees a huge government property in the distance with two statues of Malcolm X and Martin Luther King shaking hands.

"Oh, that's city hall. That's where they hold important meetings. Also, there is a history museum and farm located there. They keep public records there, hold court, do mental health assessments, and hold artifacts from the past. Man, I love that place!" Cam says with excitement. "Actually, I have some fruit for you that's from there. Reach into the back and grab the satchel and keep it. I can get more," Cam states.

Rob reaches into the back of the car and grabs the satchel that has some fruit in it. He grabs a fruit and starts to eat it.

"Wow, that's amazing, IT'S SO JUICY!" Rob says with excitement.

"Ahh, those are golden peaches, those are my favorite! They're a hybrid of peaches and oranges, very juicy and delicious!" replies Cam.

"Wow, I got to say it seems ethnics really changed the planet around," says Rob.

"Well, we tried, did a good job for the most part, but here are still people who refuse to live in peace, Asians for example. Most went back to their homeland and banned the travel of African descendants, still racists as fuck. Middle Easterns and Filipinos are still around, and we all live in harmony in spite of history, as you saw," explains Cam.

"You know, whites aren't as privileged as you all claim. We still have issues with cops and politicians and whatnot too. You all don't own disorder," Rob says.

"Privilege doesn't mean your life isn't hard. It means your life isn't harder due to the color of your skin. White have been privileged for years, everyone saw it, but the powers that be did everything under the sun to deny and hide it."

"Well, if you acted right, you all wouldn't be in so much trouble all the time," responds Rob.

At that point, Cam pulls the car to the side of the road and says, "LISTEN, MOTHERFUCKER! I don't have to help you. You sound just as racist as the history books described. This experiment is going sour real quick. Now if you want, you can walk it from here. Otherwise, I suggest, if you want my help, then shut the fuck up and sit there. And that's on behalf of my ancestors!" Cam says angrily.

"Look, I'm just saying—"

"Yeah, I know what you're saying. Say less," Cam interrupts Rob, and for the rest of the ride to TNZ, the two are silent; not long after, they arrive at TNZ.

THE NEUTRAL ZONE

The Neutral Zone is full of people; it looks like one big outside flea market under tents for walking safely under rainy days. There are people of all races here, including whites, some with collars, and some without. There are plenty of kiosks selling goods to people, performers of arts, eateries, and more; it's a wonderland for society. Cam and Rob pull up and park. After getting out of the car, Cam refreshes Rob on how to act.

"Okay, we're here. Remember, while here, do not talk to anyone, don't touch anything, and don't go anywhere without me. Stay close and follow me. Matter of fact, just keep your hands in your pockets."

"Yes, mother," responds Rob.

"Yeah, I got your mama right here. While we are here, I have to pick up a new battery for my phone," Cam respond.

"What, you didn't recharge your phone while sleeping like regular people?" Rob says sarcastically.

"Actually, we don't recharge phones anymore. That's old technology. Now we use biomass batteries that recharge themselves, even faster if you put it in the sun. But it dies after a while, so you'd have to buy a new battery every six months or so," Cam explains.

"Okay, fine, let's just hurry this up. Wouldn't want to insult you with I'm ignorance," Rob says sarcastically.

"Too late for that, motherfucker! You know, you're a real prick. I've been nothing but nice to you. Keep it up, and we'll see how long you survive without me," replies Cam.

Rob is silent.

"Nothing to say? Good, you're learning. We're almost done. Once we get to the trains, we can go our separate ways and be done with each other, and you can be among your ignorant ass people," Cam states.

The two walk through TNZ. As like the last places, Rob is marveled by the sights. There are performers doing magic, singers, arts and crafts; big screens showing honorable citizens, the time, temperature, and news; animal petting with pets of different species, llamas, lions, hyenas, dogs, camels, etc.—cruelty free.

"Okay, we're here, just give me a few minutes," say Cam.

Not too far from where the two are standing is a man preaching on a small stage. After hearing a few things, Rob strolls over to get a better listening.

"We all have heard the stories of corrupt governments and politicians from the past, corrupt cops and doctors, war on foreign land and war on their own people. We have put a stop to most of the evils of the past, but the fight isn't over! We have to fight everyday to keep a safe society, for equal rights for all. Fight for the truth beyond just being right. We must fight with ourselves! But it is the good fight, the fight that's worth it, for everyone's sake, stranger and familiars. Be honest, love your neighbors, spread love, and most importantly, love yourselves. That is the only way. Lead by example and don't be a follower of corrupt ones who use deceit to get ahead in the world. We can all evolve and prosper, but we can't do it alone, no, that's a together Job, so let's work together," the preacher rants.

Rob likes what he hears surprisingly; he agrees and claps with the crowd. As he is clapping, he looks back at Cam to see if he is done, and as he turns around again, he puts his hands in his pocket but brushes against a big African American woman in the process.

"UM, EXCUSE ME! What do you think you're doing? Police! This man just grabbed my ass!" the woman screams.

"Whoa, I never touched you like that. My elbow brushed your shoulder as I turned around," Rob replies.

"YOU LYING-ASS SAVAGE! Someone must have seen him," the lady says as she looks back at the crowd behind her, but they didn't see anything and don't know what she is talking about.

"Listen, lady, I'm sorry you think that, but I didn't—"

Just then two cops who noticed the commotion show up.

"What seems to be the problem here?" asks the first cop.

"This .. . SAVAGE...just sexually abused me," says the woman.

"What happened?" asks the second cop.

"He grabbed my ass as I was watching Jerome Kweli preaching the good word." She finishes with "Sick pervert!"

"Where's your collar or tattoo?" the first cop asks.

The cops grab Rob and instruct him to come with them in peace.

"But my hands were in my pockets. MY HANDS WERE IN MY POCKETS!" screams Rob.

Hearing the situation, Cam rushes over and confronts the cops.

"What's going on here? Why are you detaining my slave?"

"This is your slave? Where's his collar?" asks the first cop.

"He's new, his collar is still being delivered, I don't have his papers because I didn't think we'd be long or have any problems. He's very level-headed," Cam says in spite of Rob. "Good thing, he wasn't wearing a collar. This could have got very messy. Now what's the problem here?" asks Cam.

"He is being accused of sexual assault. We are taking him to check the cameras. You know you can also be charged for no papers and the responsibility of your slave?" says the second cop.

"I'm aware. I'm also aware I can take my promise to appear now and leave with him, so that's what I'll do with a promise to appear before the courts with him," says Cam.

The officers let go of Rob, pullout a tablet, and print off a summons to appear and a fine of $250. The first cop looks at Cam and tells him to request the surveillance tapes of the incident for evidence if in case it might be useful. Cam thanks him, and the cops leave them.

"I'll see you in court, SAVAGE!" the woman says as she walks away.

"Jeez, are you okay?" asks Cam.

"Yeah, I'm fine, thanks for saving me," responds Rob.

"I told you to keep your hands in your pockets. What happened?" asks Cam.

"I did. I don't know what that lady was tripping out about. I don't even like—well, you know, I mean, beautiful but not my type," says Rob.

"Good, more for me...Welcome to the new world, you racist prick, I bet my ancestors are just laughing their heads off at all this. It's really beautiful," say Cam with a smile.

"Yeah, I bet can we go now, please?" asks Rob, and the two make their way to the trains.

The train station is packed with travelers. There are eight lines of trains, two going and coming from each direction of north, east, south, and west.

"Okay, we got to head south from here. I know I said we'd part ways from here, but there isn't many passengers going south. I wouldn't want anything else to happen to you before you got to your paradise. I'll go as far as the entrance to the Savage Lands. After that, you're definitely on your own. Sorry, but I have a family to think of," says Cam.

"You know, you really don't have to do all this for me, but I'm grateful you've help me in my time of need. You're a good man, Cameron," says Rob.

"You sound like you've excepted death. That's a common feeling, I guess, for anyone going through the Savage Lands. Besides, this has been a great history lesson in real life. It doesn't get any better," replies Cam with a smile.

"Really, I don't know how to repay you," says Rob.

"Just get to where you need to go and don't come back to my shed, motherfucker!" Cam says jokingly. "Look, here comes the train," says Cam as the train pulls into the station. "You ready for this, Rob?"

"Yeah, let's get this over with," replies Rob.

The two board the train and take a seat. They are the only two people riding the train. The train is automated, so they are literally alone for the ride. As the train is pulling off, Cam's phone receives a notification.

"2000-zero-zero party over, oops, out of time (doot doo-doo, doot doo-doo).TONIGHT WE GONNA PARTY LIKE IT'S 1999," and then it stops.

"Isn't that Prince? I'm surprised you know that song," says Rob.

"Know it? It's a part of black history musically. Plus, it matches the last four digits of my phone: 834-505-1999.It's almost too perfect of a match not to do it. Plus, it's an easy-enough number to remember, right?" Cam says.

"Yeah, I'll try not to forget. 834 is the area code?"

"Yeah, then 505, worldwide service, so call me sometime, let me know how you're doing. Hey, I heard in history class you all had to pay something called long-distance plans. That's just crazy. All calls are long distance if you think about it. If it wasn't, you would just talk," says Cam.

"Yeah, I bet a lot of things from my time are funny to you all, eh? Whatever happened to Trump?" asks Rob.

"Trump? The ex-president that was publicly hanged?" says Cam.

"Never mind, I'll fill in the gaps," says Rob.

The two continue talking and laughing 'till they reach their destination.

THE SAVAGE LANDS

The Savage Lands is nothing like TNZ or King. It's a forest land for a few miles. Besides the concrete slab they have there for the train stop, there isn't nothing there, except a box, a sign showing arrival and departure times, and a damaged bench for sitting. Apparently, no one takes care of this place.

"Well, this looks comforting," says Rob.

"Yeah, sadly, it is as bad as it looks," replies Cam. "Okay, from here, you head straight south. It's about 3.7 kilometers, so you should get there in an hour or so if you keep up a good pace."

"Do you think I'll make it?" asks Rob.

"I really don't know. Hopefully, you won't run into any savages. If you do, just talk your racist mumbo-jumbo. They might just make you their leader," Cam says joking. "But seriously, be safe out there...Oh yeah, you should probably take a weapon from the weapons box," Cam adds.

"There's a weapons box?" asks Rob.

"Oh yeah, weapons aren't allowed past here. You could get shot on sight. In TNZ, if they catch you using any form of weapon, you could call it premeditated, so people leave their weapons here for anyone else who might come through. Surprisingly thoughtful, if you ask me," says Cam.

"You're kidding me, how is it so bad here but so good back there?" asks Rob.

"Well, in order for anything to exist, so must its opposite," say Cam.

Rob goes through the box and picks up a pickax with a worn-out pick, much shorter than usual pick-axes from wear and tear. It also has dried blood on it. There is a strap from the bottom of the handle to the top, making it easier to carry on your back.

"Nice, you could swing that and do some serious damage. All that dried blood shows its usefulness, I guess. Okay, you got your fruit, you got some water...Oh, I almost forgot—" Cam goes into his pocket, pulls out a compass, and hands it to Rob. "Here, use this to navigate. Do you remember what direction to go?" asks Cam.

"Yeah, straight south," replies Rob.

Looking at the forest, Cam says, "Okay, I guess you're ready to go."

"Yeah, I guess so. Thanks for everything. I really couldn't have survived without you," says Rob.

"Well, I'm sure Saint Badu will bless me with good fortune for my good deeds in time. Life is funny like that," Cam says, and the two laugh and hug.

"Okay, time to get going," and Rob starts walking off.

"GOOD LUCK, ROB, AND PLEASE STAY THE FUCK OUTTA MY SHED!" Cam says as he watches Rob walk into the forest and soon out of sight.

About forty minutes into the journey, Rob stops and checks out his surroundings and catches his breath. Behind him is a huge rock. In the distance, you can hear some people screaming from all directions, some louder and closer than others. Rob reaches in his satchel, grabs the water, and takes a few sips. After hearing the screams when entering the forest, he has been moving at a fast pace, running at times and jogging to preserve energy. Not far from where he is he hears a woman screaming for help. "Someone, please, help me!" It sounds close, so Rob goes to investigate the situation. He runs in the direction of the screams, and not long after, he stumbles upon a female tied up and clothes torn. He runs over and tries untying her.

"Are you okay?" asks Rob as he struggles with the knots.

"Thank God, you're here, mister. Some savages raped me and tied me up. Please hurry. They can come back any minute now," the Southern-sounding lady says.

"I'm trying, but the knots are—"

Just then three savages spring out of their hiding spots. It was blankets covered in dirt, twigs, and leaves, so they blended in with the environment. Rob fell into their trap. One has a pickax and in camo colors like an army brat, another is in all black with a bald head, and the last one is in torn clothes but carrying a hatchet.

"Easy there... Don't make any fast movements," the one in camo colors says.

"Jeez, took you guys long enough," the lady says as she slips out of the knots with ease. She gets up, dusts off, then pulls out a knife and puts it to Rob's throat.

"You gotta be kidding me," says Rob.

"What's in the bag?" asks the one in all black.

"Just some supplies for the journey. Listen, I don't want any trouble. I'm heading to the White Zone, and—"

"SHUT THE FUCK UP!" says the one with the hatchet.

The female tries taking off Rob's bag, but this is life or death now, so Rob punches her in the face. The one with the hatchet runs in and swings at Rob but misses. At the same time, the one with the pickax rushes in and swings but hits his friend. Rob punches him down and takes off running.

"WE'RE GONNA KILL YOU, FUCKER!" the one all in black screams at Rob, but he is too busy tending to his friends to chase after him.

As Rob is running, he looks back to see if anyone is following him. He continues running 'til he sees a fallen tree on the ground, so he ducks behind it and hides while he catches his breath. As he is catching his breath, he gazes around to see his surroundings. For no reason at all, there is a pink box with a ribbon lying there, pretty new-looking besides wear and tear of rain and weather, couldn't have been there more than a week. Puzzled by this box, Rob crawls over to it and examines it. To his surprise, there's a tag with his name on it. He opens the box and finds a phone and a note that has the words "CALL HIM" written on it.

"Wha—what the hell?" questions Rob.

In the distance, you can hear one of the savages scream out, "He went this way, keep looking, he has to be around here somewhere."

Rob puts the phone in his satchel and takes off running again.

"THERE HE IS!" says the female, and the savages take off running after Rob.

Rob is exhausted and can't keep this up much longer. He decides to make a final stand against the savages. He puts his back against a large tree and takes the pickax off his back and prepares for battle. His adrenaline is pumping. He is breathing hard and ready to kill whatever comes his way. He has entered savage mode.

"Okay, fuckers, you want me? COME GET ME!" Rob screams.

The savage dressed in all black, the female, and the one with the pickax slowly approach Rob.

"You're dead now, fucker!" the female says.

Rob gets in swinging position with the pickax held ready to swing. They rush in when, suddenly, someone screams, "FREEZE!"

Five men in all-black army gear armed with rifles appear.

"GET DOWN, NOW!" demands one of the soldiers, and the three savages take off running.

The soldiers surround Rob and begin questioning him.

"What are you doing here?" asks a soldier.

"I'm trying to make it to the White Zone. Please don't shoot me. I've had such a bad day already, but if you are going to shoot me, please don't waste my time. I'm sick of running," says Rob.

"We aren't going to shoot you. We aren't savages. We're soldiers patrolling for the White Zone. Follow us. We'll get you there safe," says the lead soldier.

"Oh, thank God, you guys are saviors, not savages," Rob says.

"Well, we gotta protect our own, right?" asks another soldier.

Rob nods in agreement and begins travelling with the soldiers to the White Zone.

THE WHITE ZONE

The White Zone is surrounded by at twenty-foot-high concrete wall with two huge double doors for an entrance. Inside, there are hundreds of white people, poor white people, with ripped clothes, dirty miserable faces, half dead, their children playing, making the best of life, people playing music on homemade instruments, chasing women like squirrels, people showing in a lake, people shitting on dug-up holes, people drinking dirty water, people fighting over food scraps, and more sad visuals. This is the hell they live in now. It's like a third-world country for our time. Rob sees all this and his heart drops to his stomach. He is disappointed in the life they chose to live. The soldiers walk him through TWZ to a big tent located at the back of this section of town. Inside, he finds their leader, a man all in black, fresh black boots, a gun in holster and a knife on the side(Woody Harrelson from *Plant of the Apes*), bald head, and tattoo of a noose down his forearm.

"Well, what do we have here?" asks the man.

"Sir, we found this man in the Savage Lands being chased by savages. He says he was on his way here," says the lead soldier.

"Tell me, why would you leave paradise and risk coming all this way through dangerous terrain?" asks the man.

"I got kicked out. Some woman claimed I sexually abused her, but I would never do anything like that. She used my race against me," says Rob.

"Yeah, sounds like something a monkey would do. You can't trust them, talking all that brotherly love but showing none to us. Really, that was a way to organize against the white man after everything we've done for them. They wouldn't be where they are now if it wasn't for us," says the man which is followed by one of his soldiers calling Africans ungrateful baboons. "Well, don't worry, now you're among your own people. Mind you, this isn't paradise, but it keeps us alive another day. We eat together, sleep together, and die together. We're like one big happy family," says the man.

Two of the soldiers are going through Rob's satchel and find the fruit.

"Sir, look at these!" he says as he pulls out the fruit.

"HOLY SHIT, IS THAT FRUIT? HAHA! GIVE ONE OF THOSE BAD BOYS HERE," says the man. The man takes a big bite of a golden peach. "Woo-wee, that's juicy! I can't remember the last time I has one of these! The niggers just let you take their fruit?" asks the man.

"Someone gave it to me, said they got if from a farm in their city hall," explains Rob.

"City hall, eh? Really, did you see it for yourself? Which building is it? I mean, they have some many wonderful monuments there," asks the man.

"Yeah, it's the big one with MLK and Malcolm X shaking hands. I'm sure they'll give you some if you ask nice," says Rob.

"Hmm, that monument is in the Township of King, if I remember correctly. Interesting. That should be my town. My name is Jared around here. I'm the real 'King,'" he says. "As of now, you are our guest here. Boys, give him back his belongings and take him to a comfy reserve house. Get him some food, and you can rest for the night. I bet you'll sleep a lot better being around your own. I have some things to take care of still, and the night is young. It's been a pleasure meeting you—um, what's your name?" asks the man.

"It's Rob."

"Rob...enjoy your stay," says Jared, and the soldiers give back Rob's satchel and lead him down the street to the north part of town where there is a townhouse complex.

Most of the houses are broken down, windows broken, spray-painted, each with a noose hanging on the front tree, and in the centre is a grass pasture with a ten-foot-tall Jesus Cross. The soldiers walk Rob to one of the houses and open the door. They also give him a key so he can leave and return as he wishes. Rob enters the townhouse and closes the door. He looks around, and it's a pretty simple design: a family room, a kitchen, a washroom, a basement, and stairs going to the second floor. He heads up the stairs where he sees three bedrooms, two smaller ones and a master bedroom, which he chooses. Inside is a big dusty mirror, broken windows, and a queen-sized bed. He lays his satchel on the bed and lays next to it. After tossing and turning for forty-five minutes, he falls asleep, never noticing the small camera in the back corner of the ceiling.

The next morning, as the sun is rising, Rob is woken up by loud bangs on the front door. He heads down the stairs and opens the door, and it is Jared with ten armed soldiers.

"Well, good morning, sunshine... You get a good night's sleep among your own?" asks Jared.

"Yeah, slept like a baby," replies Rob.

"That's good to hear. Well, I was hoping you would join me on my morning errands. You being new and all, it would be a good chance for you to see how things operate around here," says Jared.

"Sure, sure," replies Rob.

Rob locks the door and follows Jared down the road to the east part of town, where there are soldiers on top of a hill next to a big oak tree. On a branch of the oak tree is a long rope dangling to the floor. They seem to have some lady captive.

"This will only take a minute, pardon me," says Jared as he walks up the hill to the soldiers and their prisoner. "Lorain Hillman, you have been charge for theft of food and injuring a peacekeeper. Have we not been good to you? Do we not supply you with nutrients? And this is how you repay us?" says Jared.

"You know you're saving all the good meat for yourself. It isn't fair!" the woman says with a broken voice and swollen lip. She has been abused under his custody, and it's clear.

"See, that's the kind of rumors that lead to further problems, and for that, we can't have you around or let you go. You know too much, and for that, you will be silenced. Boys, hang her up," instructs Jared.

The soldiers put a noose over her head while she struggles with them, but after a few punches, she is unresistant. They fit the noose around her neck, and four soldiers put the rope from the other side and hang her until her neck snaps. Jared returns to Rob who has witnessed everything and is in total disgust.

"What did she do?" asks Rob.

"She was a thief, stole food from the plates of children. We don't allow those things around here," replies Jared.

"Don't you think her punishment was a bit harsh?" asks Rob.

"Well, that's just the role of a king, isn't it? Justice must prevail, or there will be disorder," Jared replies with a serious face. "Anyways, we got to get more meat to eat, so we're going hunting!" Jared adds, and his soldiers hollered, "woo!" repeatedly.

"Okay, this should be fun," says Rob.

The group walks to another part of town where they have trucks and a Hummer parked, all in horrible condition. Jared is in the Hummer, of course. He also has a driver. They instruct Rob to get into the Hummer with Jared, and he does. As they drive to their destination, Jared engages in conversation.

"Not sure if you're familiar with the area, but to hunt, we have to go a few miles east. We ate whatever was close to us, them buggers got smart and learned to keep their distances. It's okay, makes it more fun for us and out of the reach of the savages," says Jared.

"Yeah, I bet. That's funny, I thought we were all savages," says Rob.

"Not all of us...Most of us are pretty cool individuals and resent that title. I'm surprised you don't feel the same, brother," says Jared.

"Oh, I do. Seems judgmental, if you ask me. Seems really hypocritical too," replies Rob, and Jared smiles.

"So how was it living around those monkeys?" asks Jared.

"Scary, at first...but the more I learned, the more I wanted to be around them, you know?" says Rob.

"So what brings you these ways?" asks Jared.

"They're too racist. I could be around that for long, and fuck collars," replies Rob.

"Guess you wouldn't mind if something were to happen over there?" asks Jared grimly.

"Something like what?" asks Rob.

"Well, you said they hold their fruits in city hall, correct? I figure we should go 'borrow some,'" replies Jared while doing air quotes.

"I don't know, you don't look like the borrowing or ask-nicely type," says Rob.

"Nicely? This is survival! You know how long it's been since I had a fruit before last night? You know what our food is made of? When we can't find meat, we have to put bugs in our soup...BUGS, DAMMIT! You telling me we don't deserve to have nutrients? Are we really that bad?" Jared replies.

"I don't know, I just met you, but can't you just ask for some seeds and work something out?" asks Rob.

"We ask all the time. They say this is our punishment. They only leave bags of grains every two weeks. As shitty as that tastes, that only lasts for so long. All I'm saying is getting some seeds and fruit would be a lot easier and less messy if you just pointed us in the right direction. You won't even need a gun. You know we need this," states Jared.

"I really don't know. I was asleep for that part of the ride, sorry," says Rob.

"Okay...okay...well, you've still been very helpful. We aren't far from the hunting grounds now. Just sit tight, and we will be there in no time," says Jared, and the group is silent for the rest of the ride.

Within ten minutes, they arrive at the hunting grounds, another forest, much larger than the Savage Lands. The group park, exit their vehicles, and gear up. Three soldiers have assault rifles, and seven have bows and arrows.

"All right, boys, LET'S HUNT!" says Jared.

"WOO!" say the group repeatedly as they enter the forest.

The group walks deep into the forest in a spread-out line, about twenty feet in between. They walk slowly and as quiet as possible; no one is speaking. Eventually, a soldier spots a pack of coyotes, about nine adults and a few cubs. The soldier signals the others. "Skss-skss, skss-skss," he says in a low-enough tone that the ones near hear him and do the same sound to inform the others.

They all move in on the soldier and observe the situation. Without speaking, Jared instructs them to circle around and surround the prey. Rob stays back as the men get into position, and then they strike. Arrows are flying everywhere, coyotes are hit and trying to run, but the ones that get too far are shot. After the adult coyotes are shot dead, the soldiers walk up and slaughter the cubs. Jared and the soldiers start hollering, and with that, the hunt is over. Robs moves in and observes the scene; he is speechless.

"Okay, boys, tie'em up and carry'em out to the trucks. Sack the cubs. They have the most flavor. We're eating tonight!" says Jared, which is followed by quick successions of "woo" from the soldiers.

Jared then grabs one of the cubs from a soldier, cuts the cub's throat, and drinks its blood. "Man, that's tasty! You want some, Rob?" asks Jared with a grin on his bloody face.

Rob looks away in disgust.

"Every bit counts, my friend," says Jared.

"Yeah, I'll stick to the grains," replies Rob.

Jared smiles and hands the cub back to the soldier to put in his sack, and the group starts walking back to the vehicles to return to the White Zone. When they arrive and park, Jared instructs his men to bring the meat to the butcher, cut up half and put it in Jared's personal freezer, ground up whatever is left, and put it in a community soup.

"See that, Rob, my people will eat today. That's what a king does. You're like my little good luck charm," says Jared.

"Yeah, well, I'm glad everything worked out," replies Rob.

"Me too, me too...Say, Rob, would you walk with me for a minute?" asks King, which Rob doesn't refuse.

The two start walking toward the community, and King begins conversation. "So how long were you with them niggers? Anything you can tell me about them or even their layout?" asks Jared.

"Nothing much, just buildings and houses. They seem to have everything worked out and in order. Peaceful but closet racists, really. They won't admit it, but it's obvious...It's in the things they do, like making white people wear collars and treat them like second-class citizens. I understand why now, but...I don't know, I guess they have their reasons for all that. Besides that, it seems like a great place from what I saw," explains Rob.

"What you saw, eh? Doesn't seem like you weren't around them long. Where did you say you were from again?" asks Jared.

"Well, it didn't work out living with family, difference of opinion, ya know? Anyways, I left the country and went there thinking it might be better, it was, but it just wasn't for me," says Rob, relating it to his personal story.

"Yeah, I hear ya, family can be a bitch at times. But tell me, did you see any guards in King or the Neutral Zone?" asks Jared.

"I didn't really see any in the suburbs besides the cops, but security is in TNZ and King, got to enforce the peace, as they say now, I think," Rob says jokingly. "Why all the questions?" asks Rob.

"Oh, just trying to visualize a prettier picture than what I see daily, monkeys out of trees and in office, maybe us whites can have that again someday," says Jared.

A soldier then calls out for Jared's attention, with him are three more guards and what appears to be three savages armed with spears.

"Excuse me, I have something to tend to," says Jared as he departs from Rob and to the group.

First, it was the questions, but now this. Rob is very suspicious, so h follows them to Jared's tent and sneaks to the back. He can hear words, but they are muffled, so he moves in closer. He sneaks to the side of the tent, which is closer, and can hear what is being said clearer now.

"So if we wear our cloaks and hide our wooden daggers, we should go unnoticed. Most of us do that anyways. Just don't draw attention by causing a commotion," says a savage.

"We can't travel together, so we will have to travel in small groups of four. We can spread out and blend in at TNZ until it's time to strike. After that, we riot in King until we find city hall. Kill anything and anyone who stands in our way. We'll break in, take some fruits, and rob the seed bank," says Jared.

"Maybe we should burn the place down, make them start over again, even the odds a bit, fuck them niggers," says a savage.

"We'll just play it by ear for now. If we do, we should definitely bring down those statues. I would want that around when that becomes my town," says Jared.

"What about the cops and security?" asks a savage.

"Well, I've seen some of your people in action, masters of sneak you might say. I have faith you will be able to handle that problem when the time comes. Plus, my people will be in position by then. We will strike together and be victorious together. We will travel at night so there's less attention. Let them wake up to the surprise. Make sure your people are ready too," says Jared.

A soldier who is tired of standing in the same spot starts strolling and patrolling the parameter. He strolls to the side where he stumbles upon Rob.

"HEY, WHAT AE YOU DOING THERE?" asks the guard.

"I, uh, I'm just taking a leak, gotta go when it pinches, right?" replies Rob.

"MOVE FROM THERE NOW!" screams the guard.

"I'm going, I'm going," says Rob as he leaves the scene.

Jared hears the commotion and leaves the tent to investigate. Upon emerging, he sees Rob speed walking away. He already recognized the voice. Now he just needs to figure out what Rob is up to. He notices Rob heading in the direction of the townhouses and goes to the surveillance room to spy. Rob gets to the townhouse and runs up the stairs to the master bedroom where his satchel holding his phone is. He grabs the phone, turns it on, and tries to remember Cam's number so he can warn him.

"Fuck, okay, it's the prince song 1999, and 505, but what was the area code? 8...8...834!" Rob remembers the number and calls Cam. He hears a ringtone, and soon after, Cam answers the phone.

"Hello...Hello?" says Cam.

"Cam, it's Rob, listen, you gotta—"

"Rob? Aww, hell naw, don't tell me things didn't work out and you want to move back into my shed? Too late, already rented it out," says Cam jokingly.

"Listen, you have to warn your people. The whites and savages are planning an attack on city hall. They want the fruits and seeds," says Rob.

"Speak up, you're breaking out, figures the White Zone would have shitty reception," says Cam.

"LISTEN, they're going to attack city hall!" screams Rob.

"Did you say whites are planning an attack?" asks Cam.

"Yeah, they'll be in black cloaks and carrying daggers," says Rob.

"Shit! When did they say this is going down?" asks Cam.

"They said they are—"The phone loses its signal. "Hello...HELLO?" Rob calls out to Cam, but here is no response.

Soon after, there are loud bangs on the front door. Soldiers kick in the door and rush into the house. They find Rob upstairs and pin him to the floor. They start kicking him until ordered to stop by Jared, who spits on Rob and calls him a filthy monkey-lover traitor. Jared orders his men to carry Rob to his tent and tie him to a chair for further interrogation, which they do in an abusive manner.

Jared walks in, holding a laptop. With the laptop, he plays a recording of Rob making his phone call and informing someone of his plans.

"This is our reward after all the hospitality we've shown you?" Jared says before slapping Rob. "You think you can stop this from happening?" asks Jared.

"You're all monsters. They did nothing to you that you didn't deserve. I get it. We have some cultural differences. I had my own dislike for blacks, but they're actually good people. They've done what they can to turn this world around. You chose not to live in peace," says Rob.

"Live in peace? Like with a collar? That doesn't sound like peace to me. That sounds like farming! Those racist pricks can go to hell! Fuck the whole colorful bunch of them! Don't we deserve equality? Are we not good enough to eat a decent meal?" asks Jared.

"They tried giving you equality. Again, *you* chose this life. *You* plot and scheme and give white people a bad name. IT'S ALL YOU. It's always been. They aren't the enemy...WE ARE," says Rob.

"You know, it's really sad hearing one of our own talking like that... It doesn't sound like you're with the betterment of whites movement. I can't have you in my home spreading those diseased words, so you will be executed first thing in the morning before our raid...for good luck. And we will do it in public for all to see," Jared says with a smile.

"You're gonna hang me? Do you not see the irony here, you racist fuck? You're keeping the hatred of the past alive, not them. They're trying to move past it. That's why you're living in the trees like some animals," says Rob.

"And you think you're better than us? You come here, to my home, and we welcome you with open arms, and here you are, judging us? When they judge you, everyday for five years, you would be wearing a collar. What kind of freedom is that? We live free. We do as we please. You're just a traitor to your own race, one that's quickly making me sick. Take him to the cages, boys," Jared orders his men.

The soldiers walk Rob to the west part of town where the prison camps are. It's surrounded by chain-linked fence with barbed wire on the top, sectioned off into cages, and there are hundreds of people in there, all looking energy-drained. Rats are also running around all over the place. There are plenty of guards with rifles and batons guarding entrances and walkways. They walk Rob to a cage and put him in with the rest of the prisoners of that cage.

"Make sure you all give this nigger-lover a warm welcome," says a guard.

Soon there are a bunch of angry eyes on Rob.

"What he do?" asks a prisoner.

"He is trying to stop our plans on getting food, actual food. Apparently, he thinks we aren't good enough to eat good food. Don't you guys want some food and fruit? I don't know about you, but I'd kill for some fruit myself," says the guard.

Four of the prisoners surround Rob.

"What's your deal, buddy? You don't want us to eat? You don't think we're good enough, nigger-lover," asks a prisoner.

"Look, it's not how it seems. I was just trying to preve—"

One of the prisoners sucker-punches Rob and knocks him down. The rest soon start kicking on Rob, and the crowd cheers on.

"I don't know, should we stop it? I mean, this is the most entertainment they've had in a while," the guard asks another guard. "Still, wouldn't want a riot to break out...OKAY, THAT'S ENOUGH, BACK OFF HIM!" demands the guard.

The prisoners stop kicking on Rob and return to their resting places. Rob, beaten up and injured, stumbles as he gets up and finds a place to relax and recover. His lip is swollen, his ribs are bruised. There is a bump on his forehead and blood leaking from the side of his lip from where he got punched. For the rest of the night, he is untouched but cautious and on edge, sleeping lightly and waking up at the slightest noise. The next morning he wakes up and notices people are gathered at the gate of the cage, talking to soldiers. He notices they are letting some of them out, so Rob gets up and hobbles over to the crowd.

"Are you ready to fight for your people and your freedom?" asks a soldier to a prisoner.

"Yes, I am," says the prisoner, and he is let out of the cage and directed to join the others getting ready for war by the entrance to the White Zone.

"Hey, what's going on?" Rob asks a nearby prisoner.

"We're going to war, that's what's going on. They're recruiting soldiers to raid the Township of King," says the prisoner.

Rob then pushes his way to the front of the crowd and tries to get recruited. If he can get out, maybe he can help in some way.

"Hey, what about me?" asks Rob.

"Nah, you look too beat-up. What you do to piss off the prisoners?" asks the guard.

Another guard notices them talking and interjects, "Eh, fuck that guy, that's the traitor Jared warned us about," says the next guard.

"Fucking hell, get back, scum. Wait for your punishment to come," says the guard, and Rob does so, and the crowd pushes him back and calls him traitor.

The guards and soldiers eventually recruit half the prison population and closes the door. Rob is livid, beaten-up, and can't do nothing to stop this war from happening. Soon after, Jared walks in with a group of soldiers and approaches the cage Rob is in. They open the gate and walk in to where Rob is.

"Good morning, sunshine, you ready for your punishment? Hopefully, the good Lord will be easy on you for bringing us such valuable information, and soon we will be sucking on the nectar of the gods…but I can't trust you and let you go either. Keeping you would be a danger to my society," explains Jared.

"Yeah, this almighty shithole is really something to be proud of, huh," says Rob.

"Take him away, boys! Bring him to the tree of justice, a perfect fate for nigger-loving scum like you, don't you think?" says Jared, and his men do so.

They walk Rob to the east part of town where the big oak tree sits on top of a hill, the tree of justice apparently. As King and his men walk Rob through the crowd, the citizens start yelling insults at Rob and throwing rocks and spitting in his path. Jared enjoys what he is witnessing. They walk Rob up the hill and under the tree branch with a rope dangling of it. They put the noose around Rob's neck while the crowd screams, "KILL HIM, NIGGER LOVER, TRAITOR!"

"Do you have any last words, traitor?" asks Jared.

"Yeah, I hope you rot in hell," says Rob.

"Hell? I don't know about that. I know I'm meeting my people in TNZ and King...I hope the thought of me eating some fruit after spilling some blood is a comforting last thought for you. Malcolm and Martin, right?" King says with a smirk.

Suddenly, there is a loud BOOM in the distance, and from the direction of the gate, you can see smoke rising. Soon after, you can hear gunshots.

"What—the—FUCK—was—that? Men, stay here with the prisoner. I'm gonna go check what the commotion is," says Jared, and he and the bystanders rush to the front of town, where they find most of their people dead or injured.

One thousand Neutral Zone warriors dressed in black army gear are packed inside the gates of the White Zone; five hundred with assault rifles, two hundred with machetes, two hundred hard knuckle glove boxers, and one hundred civilians of all races with bats; clearly, the whites are outnumbered and too weak to fight back. King marches to the front of the white line of fighters; forty with guns, sixty with spears, and the rest with rocks in hand.

Jared says, "What the fuck are you, jungle bunnies, doing here?"

An African American commander steps forward and says, "I am Cdr. Elisha Tariq (imagine Michael Jai-White) of the Neutral Zone Peace Corps. You have violated the safety of our citizens. We got word of your plans to pillage in the township of King and your plans for city hall. You should know your peers are being held captive and are awaiting their individual trials."

Just then Cameron, holding an assault rifle, walks up next to the commander. "WHERE'S ROBERT?" Cam asks.

"The traitor? Well, he's about to pay for his war crimes. Just know you monkeys can't come in my home and wave your dicks around like this and expect us to bow to your almighty greatness. We haven't done anything wrong here. We just want our fair share," says Jared.

"You had your chance at that. We aren't here for that though. You're clearly outnumbered. We can make this a bloodbath, or we can come to a compromise—give us the man known as Robert," says the commander.

"FUCK YOU, I ain't giving you shit," Jared says as his men get in shooting stances.

The commander starts his chant. "Warriors, weapons ready?"

"WOO-AAH!" the warriors respond.

"Minds ready?"

"WOO-AHH!"

"READY TODIE FOR THE CAUSE?"

"WOO-AHH!" the warriors respond.

Jared pulls his knife and gun, gives a war cry, and rushes into battle. His men start shooting as well. The warriors with Cameron shoot back while Jared takes cover. The situation is quickly turned over, and the White Zones shooters are taken out. The warriors with hard knuckle gloves and machetes move in to take care of the white fighters with melee weapons. Within ten minutes, the fight is over, and the warriors of the Neutral Zone are victorious. Jared comes out of hiding and rushes in at the commander, who is eager and waiting. Jared takes out a few warriors on his way to the commander.

The commander shouts out, "SEARCH AND RESCUE, GO, GO, GO!"

A mixture of warriors get into small groups and filter through the town in search of Rob. The commander then rushes in to meet Jared. Jared eventually gets to the commander, and they engage in close-quarters combat. Jared swings his knife to slice the commander but misses. The commander knocks the gun and knife out of Jared's hands and gives him a few punches that knocks Jared off his feet. Jared grabs his gun and aims to shoot the commander, but the commander kicks the gun from his hand and, with the same momentum, spins and kicks Jared in the head, totally knocking him out.

"And you call yourself a king? You couldn't even be a janitor by how I just mopped the floor with you," the commander says.

Most of the white fighters are injured or dead; the rest have surrendered. Jared slowly regains consciousness and struggles to get on all fours. He looks around to realize he is defeated, surrounded, and outnumbered. Out of breath and panicking, Jared grabs his knife from the floor and says, "Fuck you, nigger, I'll never surrender."

The warriors surround Jared and point their guns at him.

"What, you scared to face me one on one? Scared a white man is gonna teach you a lesson?" Jared says.

"You're not worth the sweat drop. Take him away, men," says the commander as he turns to walk away.

Jared lunges at the commander and is shot by Cam. The commander gives Cam a nod, and Cam gives one back.

In the distance, someone yells out, "SIR, WE FOUND HIM!"

A group of warriors are walking toward the commander; Rob in their possession. Cam runs up to Rob and hugs him.

"You all right, man, you look like literal hell!" says Cam.

"Man, I thought I was a goner there...You organized this overnight?" asks Rob.

"Well, *I am* a part of the Neutral Zone warriors, civilian division. I sent word to the commander of what you told me, or at least what I could make out on the phone, and we all organized together. I'm really glad you called. See, it's an easy number to remember like I said. I love that song," Cam says happily.

"Yeah, I'm just glad someone left that phone there for me," says Rob.

"What do you mean, someone left you a phone? No one knows you're here," asks Cam.

"Yeah, I know, it's strange," says Rob.

"ALL RIGHT, WE'RE DONE HERE, MEN. GREAT JOB TODAY! LET'S GO HOME," says the commander.

"Hey, Rob, you can come back with me for a bit 'til you get settled in. We're gonna have to get you a collar, though, but in the end, it's a better life. Everything will work out in time. Maybe they might even give you a pass for citizenship...maybe even a *statue*!" says Cam.

Soon everyone leaves the White Zone; prisoners are taken, and the wounded are left to rot and rebuild society. If they try to retaliate, the warriors of the Neutral Zone will be ready.

OUR HERO

As Cam and Rob pass through the Neutral Zone, crowds are cheering and applauding the warriors for keeping everyone safe. People are meeting their families and are thankful to still be alive and that they are safe. On the big screens is an image of Rob. They must have taken it from the security footage as he was entering TNZ. Under his image is the headline "Honorable Citizen, Hero and Friend to All."

"Eh! Looks like they're giving you a pass. You're officially a citizen. Congratulations! No need for a collar. You're one of us now," says Cam.

"That's not so bad, but I'm not doing any speeches," replies Rob.

Soon the two are surrounded by an applauding crowd, all clapping for Rob. Even the Spanish and African cop from the beginning are there and clapping for him. Rob smiles and looks at Cam, who is also clapping for his *friend*. There is a celebration for a good while; eventually, they make their way back to Cam's home just beyond the Township of King.

"Tell you what, you can sleep in the guest room now, friend...Bet it'll feel good sleeping on an actual bed. What were you sleeping on over there? Leaves and twigs?" asks Cam jokingly.

"No, I had a bed, my own townhouse actually, just no privacy or interest in being there," replies Rob.

"Say, I never got your last name. What is it, if you don't mind me asking?" asks Cam.

"It's Cambridge," says Rob.

"Ahh, Robert Cambridge, give me a minute, I have to check on something. I don't know, play with the dog or something," says Cam as he leaves Rob in the living room of his house as he goes upstairs for some strange reason.

After a few minutes, Cam comes back down the stairs with a shocked expression on his face.

"Um, I know who left the box with the phone for you," says Cam.

"Yeah? Who was it?" asks Rob.

"It was you...," replies Cam. "Your name is already in the Citizens Databank. It also said you have a house in the Township of King, not that far from here."

Rob sits in shock for a sec, than grins with excitement

Rob says, "Well, let's go meet *me*."

The two get in Cam's car and drive to the Township of King and to the residence of Robert Cambridge. It's in the eastern part of town, a visually stunning town. They pull up to a mansion with a sign that reads, "The Cambridge Residence." Cam parks, and they exit the vehicle and walk to the door.

"You ready for this? I mean, how prepared can one be to meet himself?" asks Cam.

"Yeah, I'm ready," says Rob as he rings the doorbell.

Soon after, the door opens, and they are greeted by an African American woman. As the woman sees Rob, she is in shock, her jaw drops, and then she notices Cam and composes herself.

"Hello there. Can I help you?" the woman asks with a smile.

"Yeah, I'm looking for a Robert Cambridge," Rob asks.

With pure joy in her eyes, the woman responds, "Yes...yes, um...He's in the garden, in the backyard. You can get to it from the gate on the left side of the house."

"Thank you very much, have a great day," says Rob.

The two head to the side of the house and toward the gate.

"That was kind of awkward," says Cam.

"Yeah, I know. She kind of looked familiar though, like I knew her from somewhere. I don't know, there's something in the eyes," says Rob.

The two open the gate and enter the backyard; there, they see an old man in green overalls over a white T-shirt tending to his garden.

"Mr. Cambridge?" Cam asks.

The old man stands up and turns around. It's Rob but much older. He smiles at the two, who are in total shock.

"Good, you figured it out. I didn't know if time has changed certain events that has taken place," says Old Rob.

"Holy shit!" says Young Rob.

"Yeah, this is some strange shit right here, eh?" says Old Rob.

"You...you left the phone for me? How? No offense, but you don't look like you could survive a trip to the Savage Lands," asks Young Rob.

"No, no, I sent a carrier, had to pay a little extra for the remote location and danger involved. That spot is where I fell on my journey. Figured it was a good spot," says Old Rob.

"But what if I never found it? What if someone took it before I got there?" asks Young Rob.

"Then all would be lost, but I believe in destiny. The Rob before me didn't make the call. The world was literal hell. The streets were overmonitored by the military. Everyone had chips in their arms that told everything about you: blood type, location, personal info, records. And it had a killswitch, literally everything. Animals were dead and gone, the sea was brown, there was a shortage of food, and really, all hope was lost. Imagine the Township of King but only for the elite and the rest of the world as the Savage Lands. Needless to say, white people with power are a dangerous thing. We could and should have done better," says Old Rob.

"Well, this future seems pretty good, and we have an African American wife now? That's shocking," says Young Rob.

"You don't recognize her, huh? Will it be a shock when you figure it out? She's the love of my life," says Old Rob as he looks back at the house, and in the window, the woman, smiling, is watching what's occurring from inside. "All in due time. For now, life is brand new for you. Embrace the good in all. But there's one more thing for you to do now," says Old Rob.

"Yeah, what's that?" asks Young Rob.

"You have to wake up," says Old Rob.

"What?" asks Young Rob.

"You saying this motherfucker is dreaming of me?" says Cam as he gives Rob a weird look.

OHIO AGAIN

Suddenly, Rob wakes up in his apartment, his real apartment, and it's 6:00a.m., two hours before work. The sun is slowly rising, and his TV is on. Rob is shaken, in disbelief that everything that happened was all a dream. After a few deep breaths, he rubs his face and sighs. He is glad to be home, but then he gazes around his apartment at all the racist items he has, and Rob decides to clean up his apartment. He moves his table and rolls up the carpet. He takes the noose off the wall, puts his demonic statues and gun magazines in the trash, and takes the needle-worked art and the poster of Donald Trump off his walls. All that is left is a picture of his family, a family he hasn't talked to in a while. He looks at his home and is satisfied. He finishes with an hour to spare, so he shaves, showers, eats breakfast, and heads out to work. The bus pulls up to the stop, and it's the same African American bus driver from the day before who kicked Rob off.

"Listen, I don't want any trouble today. If you get on this bus, you have to respect everyone. If something happens, I'm calling the cops," says the bus driver.

Rob promises no problems. He also takes the time to apologize for the day before. The bus driver shrugs it off and instructs Rob to find a seat. A few stops later, the bus picks up the same gypsy woman and her sick daughter from the day before whom Rob had an exchange of words with. The two sit at the back of the bus, and the woman starts praying for her daughter again. This time Rob isn't fazed. He has more appreciation for other cultures now, but a different white male goes off on the woman.

"EH, SHUT THE FUCK UP WITH YOUR MUMBO JUMBO! It's too fucking early for this bullshit!" the man screams.

Rob stands and says, "AYE... *You* shut the fuck up! She isn't hurting nobody, is she?" says Rob.

"Screw you, buddy, she's bothering *me*...Why don't you mind your own business?" says the man.

"Say another word, I'll personally be bothering you. Now shut the fuck up, sit down, and leave her alone," demands Rob, and the white guy sits down while mumbling something under his breath.

Rob looks at the woman and gives a nod, which she returns. Rob sits down in silence for the rest of the ride, proud of himself and his heroic actions; it feels good.

Before getting off the bus, the bus driver says, "Have a nice day" to Rob, and Rob greets him back; Rob is happy.

At work, Rob is nicer to customers, enjoying each one's company, approving loans, enjoying the day. His friend Hank sends him insulting messages about customers, but Rob doesn't participate or acknowledge them. At lunch, Rob sits at his regular table, and Hank walks in and sits down with him.

"What the fuck, man? Why aren't you answering my messages?" asks Hank.

"Yeah, we got to stop that shit, it's disrespectful to people who don't deserve to be disrespected," says Rob.

"What? Are you a nigger-lover now?" asks Hank.

"Fuck off, Hank," says Rob.

"You of all people, eh? That's some funny shit," says Hank.

"I SAID FUCK OFF," demands Rob, staring Hank directly in the eyes.

"Whatever, dude," says Hank as he grabs his lunch and sits at another table.

Rob continues to eat but is soon interrupted by the sight of his African American coworker Jasmine. She has the same eyes as Old Rob's wife—it was her. She sees Rob and immediately has a look of discomfort on her face. Rob stops eating as Jasmine gets her lunch out of the fridge and pours herself a cup of coffee. Rob straightens up, stands up, and approaches her.

"Um, excuse me," Rob says.

"WHAT?" says Jasmine in understandable defense mode.

"Look, I know I haven't been the nicest person to you, I just wanted to apologize for all the asshole things I've done. There's nothing wrong with you, I'm just an asshole who didn't know better," says Rob.

"So an apology is supposed to make up for years of torment? You made working here a living hell for me, and I didn't do anything to you to deserve that. Your apology is not accepted," says Jasmine.

Hank laughs in the background.

"Okay, I understand...even if you don't accept it now, at least it's a start...it's a start," says Rob, and he walks back to his table to finish his lunch.

Jasmine grabs her stuff and leaves. Disappointed, Rob begins to eat again. At the door to the lunchroom, Jasmine has turned around and says, "Hey, Rob, it's a start, thank you" with a smile on her face. Rob smiles back, and Hank is in disgust. But Rob is *happy*.

THE END.

FUTURE PICTURES

Jasmine and Rob eating lunch together
Jasmine and Rob on a date
Jasmine and Rob on a picnic
Jasmine in a sexy lingerie outfit
Rob working with customers
Jasmine moves in with Rob
Their wedding
Honeymoon
Baby bump
Jasmine and Rob with baby in delivery room

REVIEWS

- Siskel and Ropert give this story "a pity clap."
- "He's my least favorite child," says my mother.
- "How did this get on my desk again?" asks Penguin Publishing.
- "Just what we needed," says Oakville Junkyard.

CPSIA information can be obtained
at www.ICGtesting.com
Printed in the USA
BVHW070304120920
588677BV00001B/13